DOYLE AND FOSSEY, SCIENCE DETECTIVES

The Case of the Mossy Lake Monster

(and Other Super-Scientific Cases)

MICHELE TORREY

ILLUSTRATED BY
BARBARA JOHANSEN
NEWMAN

STERLING CHILDREN'S BOOKS
New York

**My deepest thanks and appreciation to my editor,
Meredith Mundy, for her vision and enthusiasm**

STERLING CHILDREN'S BOOKS
New York

An Imprint of Sterling Publishing
387 Park Avenue South
New York, NY 10016

ISBN 978-1-4027-4962-9

Library of Congress Cataloging-in-Publication Data

Torrey, Michele.
Case of the Mossy Lake monster and other super-scientific cases
    The case of the Mossy Lake monster / Michele Torrey ; illustrated by Barbara Johansen Newman.
        p. cm.--(Doyle and Fossey science detectives)
    First published under the title: The case of the Mossy Lake monster and other super-scientific
cases.
    Summary: Fourth-graders Drake Doyle and Nell Fossey combine their detective and scientific
investigation skills to solve a variety of cases, involving a hungry cat, endangered penguins, a fish-
stealing monster, and a dirty election. Includes a section of scientific experiments and activities.
    ISBN 978-1-4027-4962-9 (alk. paper)
    [1. Science--Methodology--Fiction. 2. Mystery and detective stories.]
I. Newman, Barbara Johansen, ill. II. Title.
    PZ7.T645725Cat 2009
    [Fic]--dc22 2008047440

Distributed in Canada by Sterling Publishing
$^{c}/o$ Canadian Manda Group, 165 Dufferin Street
Toronto, Ontario, Canada M6K 3H6
Distributed in the United Kingdom by GMC Distribution Services
Castle Place, 166 High Street, Lewes, East Sussex, England BN7 1XU
Distributed in Australia by Capricorn Link (Australia) Pty. Ltd.
P.O. Box 704, Windsor, NSW 2756, Australia

For information about custom editions, special sales, and premium and corporate purchases, please
contact Sterling Special Sales at 800-805-5489 or specialsales@sterlingpublishing.com.

Manufactured in Canada
Lot #:
10 9 8 7 6 5 4
11/13
This book originally published in hardcover by Dutton Children's Books in 2002
www.sterlingpublishing.com/kids

To my husband, Carl—
three cheers for late-night
"Eureka!" moments

And to my three sons,
Ian, Aaron, and Ethan.
You know who you are
(even if I'm a little confused).
M. T.

To Loretta—
a great mom,
a close friend,
an inspirational artist
B. J. N.

CONTENTS

CHAPTER ONE

A Matter of Life or Death

It was a crisp, clear Saturday morning in the small town of Mossy Lake.

Just down the street, a little to the left, and high in an attic, Drake Doyle worked in his homemade laboratory. His hair looked as if he'd stuck his finger in a light socket. Rather messy, really, and the color of cinnamon toast. On the end of his nose perched a pair of round glasses.

Drake looked up from his microscope, his eyes a little squinty from staring so long. "Just as I thought," he murmured as he scribbled in his lab notebook.

> Just as I thought.
> Hypothesis correct.
> THEY'RE ALIVE.

As Drake slapped his notebook shut, the phone rang. (Serious scientists always slap their notebooks shut.)

"Doyle and Fossey," he answered, shoving a pencil behind his ear.

You see, Drake Doyle was his name. Science was his game. And Nell Fossey was his partner. (Besides being his best friend.) They were in business together. Serious business. Their business cards read:

> # Doyle and Fossey:
> ## Science Detectives
> call us. anytime. 555-7822

Already they had solved many cases, using their fantastic scientific and detective skills. No case was too difficult for Doyle and Fossey, the best science detectives in the fifth grade.

"Drake?" said the voice on the phone. "Drake Doyle?"

"Speaking. Who is this?"

"It's Caitlin Rae." Caitlin was in Drake's class at school. And just as Drake was the science sort, Caitlin was the cat sort. She loved cats, and everybody knew she had a bunch of them at home.

2

Every day she came to school covered in cat fuzz, and once even coughed up a hair ball.

Caitlin said, "I—I have a terrible problem."

"No problem is too terrible for Doyle and Fossey," Drake said in his most professional voice.

But instead of saying something like, "How wonderful!" or "Sign me up!" Caitlin burst into tears. She cried and cried and cried and cried and cried and *cried* and *cried* and CRIED!

Using the latest scientific techniques for hysteria control, Drake said, "Now, now," and "There, there." Ten minutes later, just as the phone receiver was getting a little soggy, Drake finally got the story from her.

"It's my cat Zappy." Caitlin sniffed. "He's not eating."

"Have you called the vet?"

"(*Sniff, sniff.*) My dad says no more vets. I have eighteen cats, and Dad says if I can't take care of them myself, then it's off to the pound with them all. He's sick of them. I didn't know who else to call (*sniff, sniff*) except, maybe, Frisco."

Great Scott! thought Drake, almost falling off his stool. If he didn't take the case, Caitlin was desperate enough to hire his competitor, James Frisco! Frisco would likely tell Caitlin something horrible. Something like, "Forget it, kid. Zappy's a goner." And then charge her five bucks anyway.

Like Doyle and Fossey, Frisco was a scientist. But he was a bad scientist. More like a mad scientist. If an experiment said, "Don't do this or that," he did it anyway. If an experiment said, "Clean up your mess," Frisco left the mess for his mother. If an experiment said, "Don't use your little sister as your test subject" . . . well . . . some things are better left unsaid.

Frisco's business cards read:

FRISCO
bad mad scientist
(Better than Doyle and Fossey)
Call me. Day or night. 555-6190

Drake could not let Frisco take this important case. "Never fear, Caitlin Rae. Drake Doyle and Nell Fossey to the rescue!"

Immediately he phoned Nell. "It's a matter of life or death. Not a moment to lose. Caitlin Rae's house. I'll pick you up in two minutes flat."

"Check."

Click.

Actually, it was more like two minutes, six seconds. As soon as Drake and his dad drove up, Nell flew out of her house and into the car lickety-split. She was never one to waste time. She was, after all, the fastest runner in the fifth grade. Not only that, Nell was a no-nonsense woman of science. Her coffee-colored hair was pulled back into a ponytail, and her scientist cap was shoved on her head in a most no-nonsense way. "Morning, Drake," said Nell, sliding into the backseat beside him.

"Morning, Nell," said Drake.

"Morning, Mr. Doyle," said Nell.

"Morning, Nell," said Drake's father.

Sam Doyle was pretty handy to have around. Especially if one happened to be a scientist. Besides driving Drake and Nell all over town, Mr. Doyle owned a science equipment and supply company. Whatever Drake needed for his lab, Mr. Doyle could get. Computers, sinks, microscopes, telescopes, beakers, test tubes—even lab coats with their names on them. It was all the same to him. "Just clean up your mess and don't blow up the lab" was what he always said. (So far, they'd only blown up the lab twice.)

Drake filled Nell in on the tragic details. "It's life or death," he said. "Zappy the Cat is not eating."

Nell nodded. "You're absolutely right, Detective Doyle. There's not a moment to lose. To Caitlin's house and make it snappy, Mr. Doyle!"

Tires squealed. In three minutes, seventeen seconds, they arrived at Caitlin's house. "Don't be long," said Mr. Doyle.

"Check," said Drake.

"Roger that," said Nell.

Drake tripped over the curb as they got out of the car. (Tripping came quite naturally to Drake.) Nell helped him up and brushed him off. She was a great partner. Together they hurried to Caitlin's house and rang the doorbell.

Caitlin answered immediately. She looked quite sad indeed, with a red, runny nose and watery eyes. Scads of fat cats wound around her legs, mewing, and several dashed outside.

"Came as fast as we could, Ms. Rae," said Drake.

"Oh! (*sob!*) I thought you'd never get here!" Caitlin pulled them into the living room and pointed to a corner. "Poor Zappy's wrapped in that blanket."

"Stand back, Ms. Rae," said Drake. "We'll take it from here."

Drake and Nell peeled away the blanket. There lay Zappy the Cat. He looked like a little bunch of furry bones.

"Hmm," murmured Drake. "When was the last time he ate?"

"About a week now. I've even tried feeding him his favorite Munch-a-Bunch-of-Mice-Bits, but it doesn't seem to matter what I put into his bowl. Nothing works."

"Why does he lie in the blanket?" asked Nell.

"Comfortable, I guess," replied Caitlin. "The blanket arrived last Saturday. A birthday present from my grandma. As soon as I unwrapped it, Zappy snuggled into it and refused to leave. And now that he's not eating—oh! (*sob!*)—I just don't have the heart to take it away."

"At least he has a comfortable place to sleep," observed Nell.

Drake nodded. Comfort was highly important for a starving cat. He rubbed the blanket between his fingers. "It's quite soft."

"Grandma knitted it from Angora rabbit hair." Caitlin sniffed and dabbed her eyes with a tissue. "Grandma sends nothing but the best."

"Where's his food?" asked Nell. When Caitlin pointed to an aluminum pie plate, Nell knelt and examined it with her magnifying glass. It was situated on the carpet about six feet from Zappy and was filled with cat food. "Certainly plenty of food," remarked Nell, standing up again.

"No reason for a cat to go hungry," agreed Drake. "This case gets more puzzling by the second."

"Indeed, Detective Doyle. Indeed."

Just then, Zappy crawled out of his blanket. His fur stood on end. Drake and Nell watched as Zappy slowly approached the food dish, ears pressed flat to his head. Closer . . . closer . . . two feet . . . one foot . . . six inches . . . one inch . . .

Suddenly, the room exploded in cat fur!

CHAPTER TWO
Simply Shocking

ZAP! MEEOOOOOOWWWWRRRRR!

Quick as lightning, Zappy zoomed past Drake and Nell and dove into his blanket. He looked rather like a speeding locomotive with claws and fur and huge eyeballs.

"Oh, poor, poor Zappy," wailed Caitlin. "That's what always happens. Oh, *booooo-hooooo!*"

"Curious," said Nell.

"Fascinating," said Drake, pushing up his glasses. "Never fear, Ms. Rae. All is not lost. Scientist Nell and I will return to the laboratory for further analysis."

"Oh, *booooo-hooooo!*"

"We'll need to take Zappy—" said Drake.

"—and the blanket—" said Nell.

"—Plus the food dish, complete with food—" added Drake.

"—for analysis," finished Nell. "Expect our report within twenty-four hours."

After listening to a few more *boo-hoos*, they piled into the car, with Zappy bundled up like a baby on Nell's lap. "To the lab!" she cried. "And make it Zappy—I mean snappy! Life or death, you know."

"Check," said Mr. Doyle. Again, tires squealed, and the smell of burning rubber filled the air.

Back at the lab, Nell phoned home. "We've got a life or death situation. Could take all day."

"I understand, dear," said Ann Fossey. And she did understand, because Nell's mom was also a no-nonsense woman of science. She taught biology at Mossy Lake University. Wildlife biology, to be precise. "I'll be here at home if you need me."

"Check."

Click.

Meanwhile, Drake pulled a book off the shelf and flipped through it until he found the right section. "Starving Cat Analysis: What to Do When Your Cat Won't Eat, and He's Snoozing on an Angora Blanket."

After Drake read the section aloud, they put their heads together. "Let's go over the facts," said Drake. And through the morning, they went over the facts and shared their observations. (Good scientists always share their observations.)

Finally, Drake said, "Based on our observations, I have developed a hypothesis."

After Drake explained, they immediately set about to test the hypothesis, which, as any good scientist will tell you, is nothing but an educated guess. They worked until just around lunchtime, when Drake's mom stuck her head around the door. "Hungry?" she asked.

"Starved," they replied.

"How do egg-and-cheese sandwiches sound?"

Nell shoved a pencil behind her ear. "Double the ketchup, hold the mayo."

"Affirmative. Hot chocolate, anyone?"

"No, thanks," said Drake.

"Just coffee," said Nell. "Decaf. Black." (In case you're wondering, real scientists don't drink hot chocolate. Never have and never will. The same goes for detectives.)

"Affirmative times two," said Kate Doyle, and she was back in a jiffy with coffee, and in two jiffies with lunch. Like Mr. Doyle, she was rather handy to have around. Her coffee was great, and her food superb. In fact, it was so superb that she owned her own catering company. (Plus, she never forgot that Nell was a vegetarian.) So you see, Mrs. Doyle was quite handy indeed.

Later, just as Nell started her third cup of decaf, and just as Drake's hair was beginning to stand on end, their hypothesis was confirmed. "Just as I thought," said Drake, shoving a pencil behind his ear. Drake dialed Caitlin's number. "Drake here. We've got your answer. Meet us in the lab. Ten minutes. Tops."

Caitlin arrived in nine minutes, fifty-eight seconds.

"Right on time," said Drake.

"And not a moment to spare," said Nell, checking her watch. "Life or death, you know."

They sat Caitlin on a lab stool and gave her a box of tissues. She wiped her eyes and blew her nose. "Can you save him? Is there any hope?"

Drake nodded. "Indeed there is. Allow Scientist Nell to explain."

Nell whacked a chalkboard with her wooden pointer. "Observe. Everything in our world is made of tiny particles called atoms. Imagine if you had a copper penny and you divided that penny in half. And in half again. And again. You keep dividing the penny until you are left with the smallest particle of copper possible. That particle is called an atom. Then, if you were to divide the copper atom, it would no longer be copper."

"Couldn't have said it better myself," Drake commented.

"Anyway," continued Nell, "atoms contain tiny particles called protons and electrons. Protons (+) are positively charged, while electrons (−) are negatively charged."

"Most of the time, Ms. Rae," Drake explained, "objects have an equal number of protons and electrons, and therefore have no charge."

"But," said Caitlin, tears brimming, "what does that have to do with poor, poor little Zappy?"

"We're getting to that," replied Drake. "Nell?"

"Thank you, Detective Doyle. When Zappy slept in the angora blanket, electrons left the blanket and piled up in Zappy's fur—"

"You see, Ms. Rae," added Drake, "Angora rabbit hair loves to lose its electrons—"

"—giving Zappy extra electrons," said Nell.

Caitlin gasped. "Poor, poor Zappy! No food and too many electrons! Oh, I think I'm going to cry again!"

Nell waited while Caitlin went through a few more tissues. (Since Nell was not as patient as Drake, this was very hard for her.) Nell tapped her foot and crossed her arms. After Caitlin blew her nose with a *honk!* Nell said, "Shall we? As I was saying, Zappy had too many electrons. This wouldn't be so bad if aluminum pie plates weren't such great conductors of electricity."

"They're quite handy, really," remarked Drake.

"Therefore," Nell said, "whenever Zappy went to eat, electrons rushed from his nose—"

"—into the pie plate—" said Drake.

"—with something rather like a miniature bolt of lightning," finished Nell. "It's called static electricity. Zappy was being zapped."

"It's simply shocking," declared Drake.

Nell whacked the chalkboard again. "Same principle as when we wear socks and then shuffle our feet along a carpet and touch a doorknob. Again, simply shocking."

"Oh, *boooo-hoooo!* Poor Zappy! No wonder he wouldn't eat," sobbed Caitlin. "I was torturing him!" Six tissues later, she said, "What now?"

Drake got up and paced around. "It's quite simple, really—"

"Yes?" Caitlin said, dabbing her eyes.

"Take the blanket away from Zappy and use a glass or plastic dish instead of aluminum," Drake concluded. "That will stop the flow of electrons, and Zappy will be just fine."

Caitlin's eyes widened. Actually, to be scientifically correct, they sparkled. (Perhaps there was a flow of electrons just then, hard to tell.) "Really?" she exclaimed. "That's all I have to do?"

"That's all," Drake and Nell said together.

Caitlin jumped off her stool and hugged them both. "Oh, thank you! Thank you! I'm so glad I didn't hire Frisco! You've saved Zappy's life! I'm going to tell everyone how wonderful you are!"

"All in a day's work," said Drake, handing her their business card. "Call us. Anytime."

That evening, Drake wrote in his lab notebook:

Case solved.
Zappy de-zapped.
Received two free tickets
to see the 4-H cat show.
Paid in full

CHAPTER THREE
A Major Disaster

The solution in the flask bubbled and boiled. It rumbled and roiled. It shuddered and . . .

KA-BLAM-O!

Waving away the smoke, Drake pushed up his safety glasses and wrote in his lab notebook.

> NEVER, NEVER do that.
> Experiment a disaster.
> Will clean up mess.

Just then, there was a scratch and a *woof!* at the attic door. "Dr. Livingston, I presume," said Drake, opening the door.

And indeed, it was. Dr. Livingston trotted in

and sat in the middle of the lab, wagging his tail and coughing a bit because of the smoke.

"Good boy," said Drake, withdrawing a blank sheet of paper from Dr. Livingston's pouch. He flicked off the overhead lights and turned on a purplish ultraviolet light. The paper glowed white. The words, however, didn't glow at all, making it easy to read.

> Detective Doyle,
> If you're reading this, Dr. Livingston has arrived as planned. Take good care of him. Look after Nature Headquarters, too. I will return in one week.
> Signed,
> Naturalist
> Nell
> P.S. Don't blow up the lab.

Drake pushed up his glasses and sighed. It was going to be a long week without Nell. She was vacationing on Penguin Island with her mother. Together they were studying penguins. Nell had taken all her homework and promised a full report to their fifth-grade class at Seaview Elementary upon her return.

"Well, old boy," said Drake to Dr. Livingston. "Looks like it's just us."

"Woof," Dr. Livingston replied.

The next day after school, Drake hurried to Nell's house. She didn't live far—just over the hill and past the park.

As Drake entered Nell's room, his glasses fogged. They always fogged because it was a little steamy. Rather like a jungle, really. It was known as Nature Headquarters. Papier-mâché trees soared to the ceiling. Vines dangled and giant leaves sparkled. Cages, aquariums, and terrariums were everywhere. There were chirps and cheeps and squeals and squeaks. It smelled like a mossy bog, topped off with turtle burps and guinea-pig poo. (If you haven't figured it out by now, Nell was, quite naturally, a naturalist. Nature was her specialty. Beetles, bats, baboons, bears, belugas— she loved them all.)

Just as Drake was tossing some salad to the gerbils, he heard Nell's voice. "*Pssst!* Calling Drake Doyle! Pssst! Are you there? Do you read me?"

Drake was so startled, he tossed a bit more salad than he'd planned. Lettuce, carrots, and cucumbers flew everywhere. Nell's voice was coming from the computer on her desk. Drake pushed aside a few leaves and ferns and turned on the monitor. There was Nell. On the screen. Large as life. "Reading you loud and clear, Naturalist Nell. How—"

"Oh, thank goodness you're there!" she cried. "I left on my Internet view camera and microphone just in case."

"Smart thinking," Drake replied in his most professional voice. He removed a piece of lettuce from the top of his head. "What's the problem?"

"It's just terrible! It's just horrible! It's just—"

"Take it from the top, Naturalist Nell, and speak slowly."

Nell wiped her face, leaving a dark, dirty smudge. Her naturalist cap was crooked, and her hair was a mess. Her raincoat and boots were covered with brownish-black goo. She stood on a beach while a helicopter whizzed overhead. "As you know, I'm here on Penguin Island with Professor Fossey."

"Check."

"Just as we began to study the little penguins, an oil tanker ran aground, and now there's an oil spill."

"Great Scott!" cried Drake, aghast. "You're right! This is terrible! This is horrible! This is a major disaster!"

And it was. A disaster. A terrible, horrible, major disaster.

"The penguins need our help," said Nell. "Observe."

The camera panned away from Nell. Beside her, using tables and plastic tubs, dozens of people were bathing oily penguins. Drake saw Professor Fossey, up to her elbows in sudsy water. She smiled and waved, flinging a few bubbles here and there. "Detective Doyle. How nice to see you again."

"Likewise," Drake replied.

"As I was saying," continued Nell, "the penguins need our help. When crude oil spills into the ocean, it weighs down the penguins' feathers. Many of them drown."

"So very sad," said Professor Fossey, scrubbing a struggling penguin.

"If they can make it to shore, we wash them," said Nell.

"But," said Professor Fossey, "no matter how much we bathe them, some of the crude oil is left behind."

"Correct." Nell nodded. "Then, when the penguins preen their feathers, they accidentally swallow the oil. Many of the penguins you see here will die from oil poisoning."

The camera focused on Nell. She looked quite serious. "But that's not all. The crude oil and the washing have destroyed the penguins' natural oils, which help keep them warm and waterproof in cold water. You see, the terrible fact is, even if they don't die from swallowing the oil, they'll freeze in these waters."

Drake slumped into a chair, unable to stand a moment longer. This was, simply put, just horrible. The penguins of Penguin Island were not only being poisoned, they were freezing, too! "What can we do?" he asked.

Nell thumped her fist for emphasis. "That's why I'm contacting you. We simply must find a solution. Doyle and Fossey to the rescue!"

CHAPTER FOUR
An Urgent Plea

Drake ran all the way home, tripping only twice.

He flew through the back door and up two flights of stairs.

"Be careful!" hollered Mrs. Doyle.

"Don't blow up the lab!" hollered Mr. Doyle.

"I will! I won't!" hollered Drake.

In the attic lab, Drake searched for his most useful scientific book. It wasn't on the shelf where he normally kept it. Then he heard a *grr!* and a *rip!* Following the sound, Drake discovered something terrible. Something horrible . . . another major disaster, you might say. For tucked away beneath Drake's desk lay Dr. Livingston, chewing on the book. "Egads!" cried Drake, snatching the book away.

Frantically, Drake thumbed to the right page. It said: "Penguin Rescue: What to Do When There's an Oil Spill and the Poor Little Penguins Are Freezing to Death." Then Drake gasped. The rest of the page was missing! "Dr. Livingston!" he said in his sternest scientific voice. "What have you to say for yourself!?"

Buuurrrp!

Drake paced the floor. "This is terrible." (*Turn.*) "Nell is counting on me." (*Turn.*) "Penguin Island is counting on me." (*Turn.*) "The penguins are counting on me." (*Turn.*) "I simply must find a solution." (*Turn.*) "Oh, this is dreadful." (*Turn.*) "What a calamity." (*Turn.*)

Drake searched the Internet. Drake asked his parents. Drake bicycled to the library and talked with the librarian. Drake phoned the environmental agencies. But no matter whom he asked, the answer was always the same: "Give the penguins a bath," they all said. "There's nothing more you can do."

After school the next day, worried as ever, Drake hurried back to Nature Headquarters. "Calling Naturalist Nell, calling Naturalist Nell. Do you read me?"

Suddenly, on the monitor, there was Nell.

Holding a shivering penguin. "Anything?" she asked.

"Negative."

Nell sighed. "I was afraid you'd say that. Ditto here. The situation is getting more and more desperate. Thousands more penguins are straggling in. And now the weather's turned for the worse." Suddenly, the wind gusted, and Nell wrapped the shivering penguin in her sweater. "I just wish I could wrap each of them in a sweater. Poor little things."

Drake blinked. "What did you say?"

"I said I just wish I could wrap each of them in a—" Nell's eyes widened. "Why, Detective Doyle, that's it! That's it! Penguin sweaters!"

"Great Scott! It's brilliant! Simply brilliant!" Suddenly, all around Drake, the crickets began to chirp. The frogs began to croak. The mice began to squeak. Indeed, everyone thought it was a brilliant idea.

"We'll have to act fast," Nell was saying. "Professor Fossey can make a sweater pattern—"

"And I'll post the pattern on the Internet—" Drake said.

"We'll need lots of help."

"And lots of yarn . . ."

After they made their plans, Drake went into action. There wasn't a moment to lose. That very afternoon he called all his friends and organized the Mossy Lake Emergency Penguin Committee. He gave them assignments and a pep talk. "The penguins are counting on us. Are we going to let them down?"

"No."

"I said, 'Are we going to let them down?'"

"No!"

"I didn't hear you! I said, 'ARE WE GOING TO LET THEM DOWN?'"

"NO!"

Woof!

The next day, an urgent plea was announced over the school intercom. It was broadcast over the radio. It was printed in the newspapers. It was posted on the Internet. "Calling all knitters! Calling all knitters! Penguin emergency!"

There was a contest at school for the class-room that brought in the most sweaters. There was an all night knit-a-thon at the Mossy Lake Senior Center. (Coffee and muffins compliments of Mrs. Doyle.) There was a televised knitting race to see who was the fastest knitter. Knitting needles were selling like buttered hotcakes. Yarn stores were open twenty-four hours a day. The Mossy Lake Moose Club volunteered to box and ship the sweaters. Dozens of them. Hundreds of them. Overnight express.

Hour by hour, day by day.

Two days . . . three days . . . four days . . . five days . . .

And then, the moment of truth.

The people of Mossy Lake stood in the town square. Breathless. Waiting. Staring at the big screen mounted on the back of a truck. Then there she was.

Nell Fossey, Nature's Naturalist.

Live from Penguin Island.

"Observe!" cried Nell. And the camera panned out. Dozens of little penguins swam in saltwater pools while wearing little sweaters. The sweaters were rather fashionable. Reds, greens, oranges, yellows, blues, and quite a few hot-pink ones. Stripes and solids. Woolly turtlenecks. Bows and ribbons.

"Awwww!" cooed the people of Mossy Lake.

"The wool sweaters keep the penguins quite warm," said Nell. "Not only that, but they can't preen their feathers and swallow the oil. And by the time the saltwater dissolves the sweaters, the

little penguins will have replenished their natural oils and will be ready to return to sea."

The people of Mossy Lake clapped and cheered.

The people of Penguin Island clapped and cheered.

The penguins waddled and dived and swam.

It was quite a happy moment, really.

Later after dinner, Drake wrote in his lab notebook.

Oil and penguins do not MIX.
Sweaters fashionable.
Penguins warm and cozy.
Payment zero.
    Paid in full.

CHAPTER FIVE
The Monster of Mossy Lake

It was a wonderfully lazy Friday afternoon. Nell Fossey lay in her hammock in the backyard and slowly sipped her lemonade. The cordless phone rang. "Doyle and Fossey," she answered.

"Ms. Fossey? Over."

"Yes?"

"Max Brewster here. Over."

"Oh. Hi, Max." Max was in Nell's class at school. While Nell tended to save wildlife, Max tended to, well, hunt and eat wildlife. On weekends Max wore camouflage. He painted his face green and brown and wore a bush on his head. But even though Max and Nell didn't always see eye to eye, Nell couldn't let that get in the way of business. She was a professional. "What can I do for you?"

"Code 47. Over."

"Code 47, you say?" Nell asked.

"Copy that. Over."

Nell sighed. "I hate to ask you this, Max, but what exactly *is* Code 47?"

"It's—it's—" And then the voice at the other end seemed at a loss for words.

"Just take it slow, Max. I've got all day."

"Roger that. You see, Ms. Fossey, this weekend's the Catch-a-Whopper-Tell-No-Lies Fishing Contest. Each day for three days, whoever catches the biggest fish is the daily winner, with the grand-prize winner being declared on Sunday afternoon. Every year I've won the five-hundred-dollar grand prize. No one else even comes close. I mean, no one. After all, I'm the best outdoorsman in Mossy Lake. Over."

"So, what's the problem? And what's the code for?"

"Like usual, today I caught a whopper. But a—a—well, a—" Max's voice dropped to a whisper "—a monster ate it. Over."

"What?" When Nell heard this, she sat up straight in her hammock. (Never sit up straight in a hammock. At least put your foot down first. And put your lemonade down, too, while you're at it.) As Nell lay on the grass staring up at her hammock, she asked, "A monster, you say?"

"Precisely. Code 47. The monster code. Over."

"Say no more. We'll take the case. Meet you at the lake in ten minutes."

"Copy that. Over and out."

Click.

Nell squeezed a fistful of lemonade from her shirt and immediately called Drake. "Mossy Lake. Ten minutes. Max met a monster. Code 47."

"Check."

Click.

While Nell rode her bike to Mossy Lake, her mind raced. Maybe it's a new species, she thought. Living in the murky depths of Mossy Lake for centuries. Undiscovered until now. She thought of all the tests she would have to conduct, and all the journal articles she'd have to write. Of course there would be interviews and public awareness meetings.

Max was already there when Nell arrived. Drake arrived shortly after, promptly tripping over a tree root. "Anything?" he asked, his voice muffled because his face was in the dirt.

"Nothing yet," replied Nell. She helped Drake

up and brushed him off. Then she opened her notebook and removed her pencil from her handy-dandy-helmet-pencil-holder. "Take it from the top, Max."

"Don't spare the gory details," said Drake as he adjusted his glasses and opened his notebook, too.

At that very moment, a ripple of wind rushed across the water, and a sudden, horrifying thought occurred to Max. What if the monster thought *he* was a fish? What if the monster suddenly appeared and gobbled him up and there was nothing left except for his boots? Then there would be no winning the contest tomorrow, because if your boots catch a fish, that doesn't count.

Acting quickly, Max picked a few more twigs and branches and added them to the bush on his head, glad he'd worn camouflage today. He felt bad about Drake and Nell, though. "I was fishing with my buddies when I caught a fish. She was this long. No, wait, she was *this* long. A beauty. Anyway, I reeled her to shore and showed all my buddies. They knew they were looking at the winner."

"And then what happened?" asked Nell.

"Just as I was holding up my fish, a monster appeared out of the water."

"What did it look like?" asked Nell.

"Slimy. Horrible. Ghastly. All of the above."

"Hmm," said Nell.

"Hmm," said Drake.

"Can you be more specific?" asked Nell. "What color was it? Did it have scales? Tentacles? Arms and legs? Did it have teeth? Bad breath, maybe?"

"Um, er—" Max scuffed the ground with his boot. "I don't know. You see, I sort of—um—sort of, well, dropped everything and ran like crazy. Everyone did."

"I see," responded Nell, quite surprised. She'd always figured Max to be a tough guy.

"And when I came back, my prize fish was gone."

"I see," Nell said again, glancing at Drake.

"Indeed," added Drake.

"Tell you what we'll do," said Nell. "We'll just talk to a few people and take a look around. Hopefully we'll spot your monster."

"In any event," said Drake, "expect our report within twenty-four hours."

"Make it quick," said Max, adding a few more sticks and twigs to the bush on his head. His eyes peeped out from between the branches. "Since I lost today's contest, I've got to win tomorrow. I've just *got* to, or else I won't win the grand prize on Sunday. After all, I'm up against a monster." And with that, Max scampered behind a bush and vanished.

First Drake and Nell questioned a few folks.

"It was slimy."

"It was horrible."

"It was ghastly."

"Did you actually see it eating any fish?" Drake asked.

"Um—er, no . . ."

Drake and Nell took notes, frowning because the answers were all the same. No one had seen what happened to Max's whopper of a fish. Like Max, they were too busy, well . . . running.

By the time Drake and Nell finished questioning witnesses and scouting around, it was past suppertime. They hadn't found much, just an old tire and a few empty pop cans. All in all, their investigation was going nowhere. "Nothing," said Nell, disappointed, putting the pop cans in her bike basket for recycling.

"Maybe tomorrow my dad can bring our boat," Drake suggested.

"Good idea. If the monster's out there, we'll find it. Five-thirty A.M. Rain or shine."

"Check."

Then, just as Nell was about to ride off into the sunset, she saw something. "Detective Doyle! Wait! I think I've found a clue." Four small plastic hoses snaked out of the water. "Follow those hoses!" Nell took out her magnifying glass. The hoses traveled away from the water and disappeared into some bushes. Nell pushed the branches aside and scrambled through.

"The hoses end here," she said, puzzled.

"And not only that," added Drake, tripping through the bushes behind her, "but the end of each hose is plugged with a cork."

"Hmm," said Nell, thinking. "I have a hunch these hoses might hold our answer. But how?" She picked up one of the hoses and pulled the cork. First she stuck the end of the hose in her ear and listened. "Nothing." She scratched it, tapped it, peered into it, bent it, stretched it, and finally blew into it. Gently, at first, then harder. And harder. It was rather like blowing up a balloon.

Drake grabbed the hose closest to him and followed Nell's example. They blew and blew.

Suddenly, in the middle of the lake, a monster appeared!

CHAPTER SIX
Code 61

It was slimy. Horrible. Ghastly. All of the above.

"Aaaaahhhh!" they screamed, dropping their hoses. They took cover, as good detectives do in an emergency.

Meanwhile, air whooshed out of the hoses, and the monster slowly sank from sight.

"Curious," whispered Nell.

"Fascinating," whispered Drake. And he scribbled in his lab notebook, drawing a chart and a bar graph for good measure.

While Drake took notes, Nell blew into the hose again.

After a bit, Drake joined her.

For the second time the monster reared out of the water. And, strangely enough, when they released the hoses, the monster sank. Up. Down. Up. Down. Definitely a pattern.

"My suspicions are confirmed," said Nell, letting go of the hose.

"Ditto," said Drake, feeling woozy. He reeled about a bit. "We must return to the lab."

"For final analysis," said Nell.

And so to the lab they rode as fast as their legs could pedal. (Even so, it took a while longer than usual because occasionally Drake would ride in a dizzy circle.)

At the lab, Drake pulled a book off the shelf. He turned to the page titled "Code 47: What to Do When a Slimy, Horrible, Ghastly Monster Snatches Your Prize-winning Fish."

Meanwhile, Nell called her mother and got permission to stay extra late. Then they chatted for a bit as mothers and daughters often do. Nell hung up the phone. "Guess what?" she asked Drake. "My mom said Frisco won today's fishing contest."

Drake frowned. "That's weird. Everybody knows Frisco can't catch a minnow, much less a—" Suddenly, he stared at her. "Great Scott! Frisco's behind all this!"

"We've no time to lose," said Nell, her mouth in a firm line. "He's up to his old tricks again."

Together they pored over the book. And after a quick supper of macaroni and cheese, with fudge tarts and sliced pears for dessert, they began to work on their plan. . . .

A monstrous plan, you might say.

At five-thirty in the morning, while the little town of Mossy Lake still slept, Drake and Nell stood at the water's edge. Mist hung over the lake, and everything looked just a tad creepy. (Drake's dad was sitting on a log, keeping an eye on things, and looking just a tad sleepy.)

"Ready, Scientist Nell?" asked Drake.

"Ready as I'll ever be." Nell snapped on her life preserver, grabbed an oar, and climbed into the boat. They pulled away from shore, rowing and rowing, until they reached the center of the lake, a little to the left of where they'd seen Frisco's monster.

And there they lowered their secret weapon. Code 61.

"Done," whispered Drake.

"Roger that," whispered Nell.

Back on shore, they helped Mr. Doyle tie the boat on top of the car and unload their bikes. Then they waved good-bye and took positions.

"Position number one, ready," whispered Nell.

"Position number two, ready," whispered Drake.

And then they waited. But not for long.

At precisely 6:27, the fisherfolk started to arrive. Now, in case you're wondering, fisherfolk come in all sizes. Tall, short, skinny, fat, and everything in between. They tend to wear fishhooks in their hats and carry coolers. Soon the lake was filled with fishing lines and fisherfolk drinking sodas.

At precisely 9:12, Nell got an itch.

At precisely 11:17, they ate some cheese-and-cucumber sandwiches and drank their emergency-ration lemonade.

At precisely 1:59, Drake fell asleep, snoring just a wee bit.

At precisely 4:02, Max Brewster yelled loud enough for everyone to hear, "Whoo-ee! I've got a whopper here! I'm reeling him in!"

At precisely 4:02½, the monster reared out of Mossy Lake.

"Aaaaahhhh!" screamed the fisherfolk, scrambling to get away.

"Drake!" screeched Nell. "Code 61! Code 61!"

"Huh?"

Once Drake finally woke up, he and Nell blew into their hoses as planned.

Then *another* monster rose out of Mossy Lake! Even slimy-er. Horrible-er. Ghastly-er. (Code 61. Monster Meets Monster.)

Suddenly, out of the bushes burst Frisco and his friends, running away as fast as their legs could carry them. "Aaaaaahhhhh! A real monster! Aaaaaahhhh!" Away from the lake they scampered, disappearing into the distant hills.

Later that evening, Nell and Drake explained everything to Max and his buddies. "You see," said Nell, "the monster was operated by Frisco and his friends."

"Simply put," said Drake, pushing up his glasses, "Frisco wanted your fish—"

"—so he could win the contest," added Nell.

"But he's a lousy fisherman," said Drake.

"Hence the monster," explained Nell. "Made it himself. It scared you silly, of course. When you ran away, Frisco snatched your fish."

"But," asked Max, "how did the monster float up and down like that?"

"Good question," replied Nell. "I was getting to that. You see, most of the time the monster was filled with water. That made him heavy."

"Quite heavy indeed," agreed Drake. "The monster remained on the bottom of the lake because he was too heavy to float."

"But," continued Nell, "there were empty balloons inside the monster. Whenever Frisco and his friends blew up the balloons—"

"—by blowing into the hoses—" explained Drake.

"—the air in the balloons pushed the water out of the monster through holes. Suddenly, instead of being filled with water, the monster was filled with *air* and rose to the surface," said Nell proudly. "Then, by letting the air out of the balloons, the monster filled with water again until it sank."

"Brilliant, if I do say so myself," added Drake. "Dastardly, but brilliant. It's the principle of buoyancy. It's how submarines operate."

Max shook their hands. "Whatever it's called, I couldn't have solved the mystery without you. I'll let you have my prize fish as payment. After I win, of course."

"Thanks just the same," said Nell. "Vegetarian, you know."

"I accept," said Drake. "My dad loves fish."

Nell handed Max their business card. "Call us. Anytime."

CHAPTER SEVEN

An Evil Plot

It all started on a Monday night.

Drake Doyle was fast asleep at his desk when the phone rang. He fumbled for the receiver. "... Earth to Mars," he said sleepily. "Come in, Martian Ambassador ... I mean, Foyle and Dossey, Er. I mean, Doyle and Fossey."

"Is this Drake? Drake Doyle?"

Drake sat up straight. Sleepy as he was, it was important to sound professional, especially after dreaming about Martians. "Speaking," he replied.

"Well, this is Alexandra Landsright. And I simply *must* have your help. I repeat: *must.*"

At that very moment, Drake's heart skipped just a little. You see, in Drake's scientific opinion, Alexandra was the most beautiful girl in the fifth grade. (She was, in fact, a beauty queen, or rather, a beauty princess. Winner of the Miss Junior Mossy Lake title for two years in a row. So it was only natural that Drake's heart would skip just a little.) "What seems to be the problem, Ms. Landsright?"

"As you know, I'm running for class president," said Alexandra. "And the election is on Friday."

"Don't worry. You have my vote."

"I'm counting on it. But there's a problem. A big problem." Her voice sank to a whisper. "Someone is plotting against me. Me! Beauty Princess Extraordinaire!"

Once again, Drake's heart skipped a beat. This sounded serious! "What do you mean?"

"My campaign posters. They're ruined. Every one of them. Today after school, someone wrote all over them with a black marker."

"Great Scott!" gasped Drake. "That's terrible!" All last week and all day today, Drake had admired Alexandra's posters. VOTE FOR ME! the posters proclaimed. VOTE FOR ALEXANDRA LANDSRIGHT! THE MOST GLAMOROUS, FABULOUS GIRL IN THE WORLD! In the center of each poster was a dazzling photo of Alexandra. They were, in Drake's scientific opinion, terrific posters.

48

Alexandra was saying, "Now my photos have mustaches and black teeth. *Who* would vote for a girl with a mustache? I repeat: *WHO?* Oh, dear me! I mustn't cry or I'll smear my mascara!"

Drake's mind raced. "Isn't James Frisco running against you?"

"Why—why, yes he is. I hadn't thought of that. Oh Drake, you simply *must* get to the bottom of this. I repeat: *MUST.* I'll pay anything. I'm desperate to win!"

"Never fear. Doyle and Fossey will catch the nasty culprit, whoever it is. You have my word." Late as it was, Drake immediately phoned Nell.

"Doyle and Fossey," she said after the first ring.

"An evil plot is hatching," said Drake, and he filled her in on the details. "We must investigate tomorrow at school."

"No doubt Frisco's behind it all," replied Nell.

"Agreed. This is our chance to catch our archrival at his dirty tricks," answered Drake.

"Check."

Click.

The next morning, Drake, Nell, and Alexandra examined the posters. Sure enough, the beauty princess was now missing a few teeth and had a mustache. Sometimes she even had a black eye or a beard. Definitely not presidential material.

"Terrible," murmured Drake.

"Horrible," murmured Nell.

"*Who* would do such a thing?" cried Alexandra. "I repeat: *WHO?* And to *me?* I repeat: *ME!* Beauty Princess Extraordinaire!"

"Hmm," said Drake, thinking hard. "Ms. Landsright, I have come to the conclusion that you must make more posters. Immediately, if not sooner. I want them hanging by the time the bell rings this afternoon."

"More posters?" asked Alexandra, frowning. "But why? They're an awful lot of work, you know."

Drake shoved his glasses up with his finger. "So we can set up surveillance and catch the culprit in the act, that's why. After all, we're Doyle and Fossey: Science *Detectives.*"

"Emphasis on the *detectives,*" added Nell.

Alexandra tossed back her golden hair and sighed. "Oh. Very well, then. I'll get my campaign manager to do it. Couldn't possibly do it myself. Might break a nail."

"Quite right," agreed Drake.

"Who's your campaign manager?" asked Nell.

"Why, Haley Glibb, of course. The most

fantastic campaign manager a beauty princess could have. I repeat: *fantastic.*"

Haley was also in their class. Just as Drake and Nell were the science sort, Haley was the politics sort. Not only did Haley wear red, white, and blue every day, she also waved flags while shouting "Hurrah!" and other such political stuff. Drake jotted a note to himself. *Haley Glibb—campaign manager.*

Just then, Haley herself came up and shook their hands. "I must say, I'm stunned," she said. "Absolutely stunned that anyone would dare disgrace an election like this. The dignity and honor of the entire political system is at stake. Tell me, what have you come up with so far?"

"Nothing yet," said Drake. "However, Ms. Glibb, I am curious about something . . ."

"Yes?" asked Haley.

"Who's Frisco's campaign manager?"

"That's easy," answered Haley. "It's Bubba Baloney Mahoney."

Alexandra added, "Everyone knows they're good friends."

"This confirms my suspicions," murmured Drake as he scribbled in his lab notebook.

"Ditto," murmured Nell as she scribbled.

"I'm afraid we must skip class this afternoon," said Drake. "Surveillance, you know. Top priority."

"Check," replied Nell. "All in the name of science."

So, following lunch, they hid beside lockers and peered around corners. They watched Haley Glibb pin up new posters. They spied while Alexandra said things like, "A little higher" or "More to the left" or ... (*sigh*) ... "Aren't I just so *beautiful*?"

And then they waited.

And waited ...

At 3:25, the bell rang. School was out. Bubba Baloney went out one door while Frisco went out another.

"You follow Frisco," whispered Nell. "And I'll follow Baloney."

"Check," whispered Drake.

Drake came prepared for such detective work. Whenever he was on assignment, he carried his detective kit. It was filled with handy gadgets like night-vision goggles, a periscope, a compass, specimen jars, a flashlight, code breakers, and a camera disguised as a teddy bear. He donned his fake glasses (complete with plastic nose and mustache) and pulled his hat down. Already he'd called his parents to say he'd be home late. Very late.

He scurried across crosswalks. He slithered behind trees. He scampered under bushes. He slid between lawn chairs. And every now and then, just to be certain he wasn't recognized, he walked with a limp. All the while keeping Frisco in his sight. It was detective work at its best. (Once, he even slipped in a dog pile but was up and after Frisco in a matter of seconds. Remember—detective work can be perilous. Absolutely perilous.)

He tailed Frisco all afternoon, spying on everything Frisco did. Frisco littered. Frisco kicked cats. Frisco stole candy from babies. Frisco crossed streets on the DON'T WALK flashing red light. Frisco . . . well . . . you get the idea. It was well past the time that school closed for the day when Drake finally called it quits. At home and following a quick supper of meatball surprise, he called Nell. "Anything?"

"Nothing."

"Ditto. The school doors open at eight o'clock in the morning. Have Alexandra meet us there at 7:55 sharp. That way neither Frisco nor Baloney can mark up the posters before we get there."

"Check."

Click.

CHAPTER EIGHT

A Secret Formula

On Wednesday morning, Drake and Nell hurried to school.

Alexandra was already waiting outside the front doors. She tossed her golden hair while her radiant smile reflected the morning sunlight.

Blinded, Drake stumbled over the curb and fell *splat!* at her feet.

"Oh, my!" exclaimed Alexandra, putting her hands over her dimpled cheeks.

"Sorry," Drake mumbled.

Nell just sighed and rolled her eyes.

(If truth be known, this was an extra-*extra*-challenging case for Nell Fossey. All this nonsense about beauty princesses, mascara, and dazzling smiles was starting to get to her. What Nell really wanted to do was punch Alexandra Landsright square in her pert little nose, but that wouldn't be very scientific at all. Instead, Nell helped Drake up and brushed him off.)

As soon as the school doors opened, they rushed in to check the posters.

"Aaaaahhhh!" screamed Alexandra.

"Great Scott!" exclaimed Drake.

"Oh, no!" cried Nell. "This is awful!"

And it was. Awful, that is. The posters—every single one—were ruined. Simply ruined. Black teeth and mustaches everywhere.

Just then Frisco and Baloney walked by. "Gee, Alexandra," Frisco said with a wink, "you look really good in a mustache."

"Yeah," said Baloney. "Don't you think you should go to the dentist before *all* your teeth fall out?"

Alexandra groaned. "See what I mean? I'm ruined! I'll never win!"

"But it doesn't make any sense," Nell said, looking puzzled. "We followed Frisco and Baloney until after school closed for the day, and they didn't come near the school."

"Hmm," said Drake, looking equally puzzled.

Once Alexandra had gone to class, Drake and

Nell found the janitor. They asked him if he'd seen anything suspicious.

"Can't say that I have," he said, pushing his broom. "Course, lots of kids stay after school. They do sports, projects, maybe a test or two. Can't keep track of everyone."

"You don't remember anyone marking up the campaign posters?" asked Drake.

"Posters? What posters?" The janitor looked to where Drake was pointing. "Jeepers! She's an ugly one! Now, what were you saying?"

"Never mind," said Drake with a sigh.

Nell handed the janitor their business card. "Thanks for your time. Call us if you see anything."

Then they walked back to class together, looking just a little glum. "This calls for drastic measures," said Drake suddenly, putting his fist in his hand. "Meet me at the lab after school." (Drake didn't know what those drastic measures would be, only that they had to be drastic.)

After school at the lab, Drake pulled a book off his shelf and thumbed through until he found the right page. "Evil Plots: What to Do When Campaign Posters Are Ruined and the Election Is Coming Right Up."

Nell sat next to Drake, and together they read the section. Then they looked at each other. "Let's get to work," said Drake.

First Nell called Alexandra. "Quick. We need more glamour photos. Drop some off at Drake's house so we can make new posters for you."

Alexandra sighed. "New posters? Again?"

"I assure you it's quite necessary. Tell no one."

"You're the boss."

Click.

Without waiting for the photos, they immediately set to work. They pulled on surgical gloves.

Snap!

And when the doorbell rang, Nell quickly grabbed the photos. "Thanks! Bye!" she said, closing the door in Alexandra's surprised face. There was simply no time to waste. Back in the lab, they worked and worked until finally they were ready.

They pulled off their surgical gloves.

Snap!

"That should do it," said Drake, nodding with satisfaction.

"Tomorrow at school," said Nell, her mouth in a thin line. "Be there."

On Thursday morning, Drake and Nell hung the new posters. Again, they were careful to wear surgical gloves. When school was finally out, they didn't follow Frisco or Baloney. In fact, they went to the lab for a relaxing afternoon of experiments. Why? you ask. Because there was no need for surveillance. . . .

The next day was Friday. Election day.

Sure enough, black teeth, black eyes, mustaches, and beards were plastered all over the posters.

Alexandra stamped her foot. "I thought you were going to get to the bottom of this!" she screeched.

Drake plugged his ears. (He had no idea that beauty princesses could screech so loudly.)

Once she stopped screeching and stamping her foot and turning purple, Drake said calmly, "I assure you, Ms. Landsright, it's all part of the plan. Doyle and Fossey, Science Detectives, will nab your culprit in plenty of time for the election, never fear. Now, here's what I want you to do . . ." And he lowered his voice to a whisper.

Afterward, Drake and Nell marched to the principal's office and received permission from Mr. Hong to carry out the rest of their plan. (Mr. Hong wanted to catch the bad guys just as much as they did. "Do what you have to do," he said, shaking their hands. "The full resources of the school are yours.")

That afternoon, all the students filed into the gym. Nell and Drake sat in the first row. Haley Glibb sat beside them. Her fingers were crossed. The row of student candidates sat facing them.

The hour wore on. There was speech after speech. Speeches for wannabe treasurers, secretaries, and vice presidents. Finally, it was time for the presidential speeches.

Frisco was first. "I promise to be a good president. There'll be no more homework, no more tests, and everyone will get A's from now on. So," he said with a smirk, "vote for me. Frisco. Because I said so." And he sat down to sounds of cheering and applause.

Then Alexandra stepped up to the podium.

And everyone giggled. (Except Alexandra, Drake, Nell, Haley, the teachers, and the principal, of course.) Alexandra cleared her throat and flipped her glossy hair. She then gave a rather nice speech about how she would make a good president, bring beauty to the school, and all of that. "And finally, to conclude, I would like to call on Doyle and Fossey, Science Detectives."

"Thank you, Ms. Landsright," said Drake and Nell. Together they took center stage.

"Hey, wait a second," said Frisco, looking confused. "I don't think that's allowed. Is that allowed?"

Drake ignored him and spoke into the microphone. "Drake Doyle here. As everyone knows, an evil plot was hatched this week at Seaview Elementary. It was politics at its dirtiest. Doyle and Fossey, Science Detectives, were hired to handle this most difficult case. Ms. Fossey?"

"Thank you, Detective Doyle." Nell cleared her throat. "Our mission, of course, was to find out who was ruining Ms. Landsright's posters."

"So we set up surveillance," continued Drake. "Only, it didn't work."

"Not even close," said Nell.

"So we were forced to take drastic measures," said Drake.

"Is this going somewhere?" Frisco whispered from behind them. "Or should I get some sleep?"

"As I was saying," said Drake, ignoring Frisco, "we took drastic measures. We made twenty new posters, lickety-split. But they weren't ordinary posters."

"Not ordinary at all," agreed Nell.

"We coated them with a secret formula. To be precise, we coated them with ultraviolet thief-detection powder," said Drake proudly. "A powder used by detectives everywhere to catch thieves."

Nell looked out at the audience. "It all has to do with light. You see, there are different levels of light. There is light you can see, and light that is invisible to the human eye."

"Meaning, of course," said Drake, "that you can't see it."

"Precisely. Ultraviolet light is light that you can't see. Ultraviolet thief-detection powder absorbs ultraviolet energy and—"

"—when exposed to ultraviolet light," continued Drake.

"—releases that energy in the form of light you *can* see," finished Nell. "This is called fluorescence."

"So what?" Frisco asked, yawning loudly. "Does anyone care?"

Nell turned toward Frisco while speaking carefully into the microphone. "Perhaps you will care when we flip out the lights."

"Huh?"

"Cut the lights!" ordered Nell.

Suddenly, the room was plunged into darkness.

Everyone gasped. And then, a great, scary silence settled over everyone.

Finally, Drake spoke into the silence. "Whoever marked up the posters is in this room. They don't know it, but they are covered with ultraviolet thief-detection powder. In just a few seconds, we will turn on an ultraviolet light."

"And whoever it is," said Nell, "will glow like a glowstick."

"Ultraviolet light, please!" ordered Drake.

And from behind Drake and Nell, a purplish light turned on.

It took only a moment before the culprit was revealed.

Drake gasped.

Nell gasped.

Mr. Hong gasped.

Alexandra gasped.

Haley gasped.

In fact, Haley gasped extra loudly because she was the one glowing like a glowstick. She jumped to her feet and pointed a glowing arm at Frisco. "He paid me!" she shrieked.

"Shh!" hissed Frisco. "You're ruining everything!"

"I'll take it from here," said Mr. Hong. "To

the office. Both of you." And out of the gym he marched, holding Frisco and Haley by the arms.

After that, the lights came on. Order was restored. The election proceeded. And Alexandra won by a landslide.

"Congratulations on your election victory," Drake said later, handing Alexandra his business card. "Call us. Anytime."

"Oh, thank you," she gushed. "You were awesome. Who'd have thought it? Haley. Of all people. Naturally, she was jealous of me." Alexandra tossed her hair and smiled quite dazzlingly. "Most people are."

"All in the line of duty," said Drake, his heart pitter-pattering.

Nell rolled her eyes. "I think I'm going to be sick." And indeed, she looked rather ill.

Later at the lab, Drake wrote in his notebook, sighing just a little as he did so.

Evil plot crushed forever.
Order restored.
♥ Alexandra ♥ the Winner.
Received one autographed
8 x 10 glossy photo.
    Paid in Full.

Activities and Experiments for Super-Scientists

Contents

Your Own Lab

As an amateur scientist, it is handy to have your own work space or laboratory. This can be as simple as a table in the laundry room or a desk in your bedroom. By following these simple steps, you can equip your lab with some essential tools, just like Drake and Nell's!

1. You will need a lab notebook. A spiral notebook works fine. Record everything in your notebook: your hypothesis, your procedure, your observations, your results—even your flubs!

A good lab notebook contains
1) experiment title
2) method (what you plan to do)
3) hypothesis (what you think will happen)

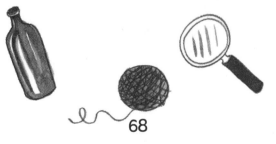

4) procedure (what you did)

5) observations (what you saw)

6) results (what actually happened)

2. Find a lab coat. Lab coats protect your clothes and skin from chemicals. (Plus, they're spiffy.) Large, white, button-down shirts with the sleeves rolled up work well. If you can't find one around your house (ask first!), they're available at secondhand clothing stores. Write your name on it using a permanent marker.

3. Keep a sharp lookout for equipment. For example, start collecting different sizes of bottles and jars (both plastic and glass), different sizes of corks and rubber stoppers, cotton balls and cotton swabs, wire, tubing, balloons, duct tape, a magnifying glass, string . . . anything you might need for an experiment. (Make sure you ask before taking.)

4. All good scientists label everything they're working on. Keep a roll of masking tape and a marker on hand for labeling.

Congratulations! You are now an official amateur scientist genius!

Good Science Tip

Read through the instructions and set out all needed materials before beginning the experiment. Use only clean equipment. Record each step of the experiment's procedure in your lab notebook.

Method to the Madness

In the story "A Matter of Life or Death," Drake and Nell used the **scientific method**. Based on their observations of Zappy, they developed a **hypothesis**. A hypothesis is a scientist's best guess as to what is happening. Like all good scientists, Nell jotted the hypothesis in her lab notebook. It might have looked like this:

> Based on our observations, we believe Zappy is gaining extra electrons from the angora blanket, then transferring the electrons to the aluminum pie plate through his nose.

After a scientist develops a hypothesis, the hypothesis must be proven. The scientist must conduct experiments, following a **procedure**—step-by-step instructions. While sometimes a scientist follows a set procedure, other times a scientist creates new steps, going beyond what has been done before. In your experiments, you will follow a set procedure. So sharpen those pencils and get ready to go!

71

The Truth About Zappy: Static Electricity

As a good scientist, you will doubtless want to know the truth about Zappy. (Oh, the truth is quite awful, but you probably want to know just the same. After all, scientists are a curious sort.) You wonder: just how badly did Zappy suffer?

The following activity will help you understand the power of static electricity. (No wonder Caitlin cried and cried and cried and cried and cried and *cried* and *cried* and CRIED!)

Beware. It's a terribly sad activity.

MATERIALS

- aluminum pie plate (small ones work best)
- blown-up balloon
- your hair
- box of tissues

PROCEDURE

1. Set pie plate on a table. (Think food dish.)

2. Rub the balloon in your hair until your hair stands on end. (This works best on cool, dry days with clean, grease-free hair. Hey—all you grunge-heads out there . . . take a hint!)

3. Your balloon is now charged with extra electrons in the form of static electricity. (Think Zappy. Think pink, tender schnozzola.)

4. Bring the balloon close to the pie plate—two inches . . . one inch . . . (Sudden exchange of electrons! ZAP!)

5. Poor, poor Zappy! Dab your eyes with a tissue and blow your nose.

6. If you can stand the sadness, go into a dark room, wait one minute for your eyes to adjust, and try the experiment again. You can actually see the sparks.

Good Science Tip

All good scientists observe carefully. They record what they see and everything that happens in their experiment, whether or not they believe it's important. Sometimes what they think isn't important turns out to be the key to the puzzle! Here's an activity you can do to sharpen your observation skills: Examine an ordinary leaf with a magnifying glass and write down ten things you observe about the leaf. (Example: tiny hairs, different colors, a soft texture.) You will be surprised at how many things you can observe when you try!

Just for Penguins: Oil Spills

If you're a penguin, oil spills spell *disaster*. And if you happen to be a penguin who can spell D-I-S-A-S-T-E-R, you're very smart indeed. For this experiment, pluck a couple of your penguin feathers and get ready to see the effect that oil has on them.

MATERIALS

- two small bowls
- 1 tablespoon water
- 1 tablespoon vegetable oil
- two downy-soft feathers*

*Note: Craft stores carry feathers. Don't use feathers that you find outside—they may carry germs that cause disease.

PROCEDURE

1. Pour water into one bowl. Pour oil into the second bowl.

2. Dip one of the feathers into the water. Take it out and blow on it gently until it dries.

3. Dip the second feather into the oil. Take it out and blow on it for about the same length of time as before.

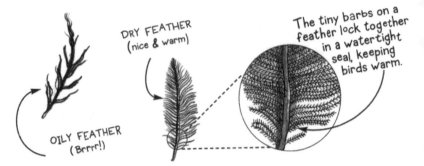

DRY FEATHER
(nice & warm)

OILY FEATHER
(Brrrr!)

The tiny barbs on a feather lock together in a watertight seal, keeping birds warm.

4. Now answer this question: Which would you (a penguin) rather swim in—oil or water?

Answer: Water. If you missed this question, read the penguin chapters again.

How Can I Help?
While there's not much you can do to prevent an oil tanker from running aground, you can still help. The surprising fact is, most of the oil in our oceans comes from motor oil that is dumped down the storm drain. If your parents change their own

car oil, ask them to try to recycle the oil through your local recycling center or auto repair shop.

Did you know?

Did you know that Drake and Nell's idea for the penguin sweaters is based on a true story? In 2000, there was an oil spill off the coast of southeast Australia, near Phillip Island. The tiniest penguins in the world live on Phillip Island and were endangered by the oil spill. Thinking quickly and creatively, workers dressed the penguins in doll sweaters. Soon sweaters knitted by people from all over the world poured into Phillip Island, and the little penguins were saved! For more information, see:

> www.penguins.org.au
>
> www.factmonster.com/spot/penguinsweater.html
>
> www.adorablog.org/penguins/index.html
> (Full of cool pics of sweatered penguins!)

Monster Attack: Buoyancy

The Scene: You are camping with your family beside a lake. The birds are chirping. The squirrels are scurrying. The flowers are blooming. All in all, it is rather peaceful. Your family goes fishing, hoping to catch a fat trout for dinner. Suddenly, a monster rears its ugly head! It's slimy. Horrible. Ghastly. All of the above. Your family screams and scampers into the hills.

The Secret: You're the culprit! Yes, you! You were sneaky. Sly. Crafty. All of the above. Using the principles of buoyancy, you constructed a monster just like Code 61. Here's how:

MATERIALS

- empty 2-liter plastic bottle
- scissors
- 12 quarters
- duct tape
- large balloon

- several long twist ties
- 12 feet of plastic or rubber tubing from a hardware store, approx. ⅜ inch in diameter
- string
- Halloween monster mask
- small cork (optional)

PROCEDURE

(Hot tip: Practice this first in a bathtub to make certain everything works.)

1. Lay the bottle on its side. Ask an adult to help you cut four holes in the bottle—two on the top side, and two on the bottom side. (If someone asks you what you're doing, say, "Oh, nothing really. Just an experiment on buoyancy.")

2. Stack the quarters into three piles and tape each pile to the bottom of the bottle, in line with the two bottom holes. These are your weights. (If you're broke, use three rocks of similar weight.)

3. Slip the mouth of the balloon over one end of the tubing. Wrap a twist tie around both the balloon and the tubing. Twist the two ends of the twist tie together until the seal is extremely tight. Check the tightness by blowing into the other end of the tubing. If the seal leaks, use several twist ties.

4. With the tubing still attached, insert the uninflated balloon through the mouth of the bottle. (Tubing will extend out of the mouth of the bottle.)

5. Use string to tie the monster mask securely onto the bottle.

6. When no one is looking, submerge the bottle in the lake. Make certain there are no air bubbles in

either the bottle or the mask. Keep hold of the
end of the tubing.

7. Hide the end of the tube behind the bush.

8. Join your family around the campfire, roast a
few marshmallows, and act casual.

9. When your family goes fishing, pretend you
have to . . . well . . . you know. Anyway, hide
behind the bush.

10. Inflate the balloon by blowing into the tubing.
(You may not be able to blow up the balloon
with one puff of air. Just hold your finger over
the end of the tubing between breaths.)

11. Once the balloon is filled, either hold your finger over the end of the tube or stick a cork in it.

12. As your family sees the monster rising from the deep, scream something monsterish like "AARRGGGG!" or "GRRRRUURRR!"

13. To sink the monster, pull the cork from the tubing or remove your finger.

14. Pretend it wasn't you.

Write a Secret Message: Ultraviolet Light

Warning! Warning! Your archenemy is lurking outside your door. You must send a secret message to your fellow detective or all is lost. You write your message. You send it "special delivery" right out the door and into the enemy's hands.

But, never fear, all is not lost. Instead of reading your secret message, your archenemy says, "Rats! It's just a blank piece of paper." And he lets your messenger go. The day is saved.

(Of course, only you and your partner know the real secret. Read on to find out how it's done. Once again, this is detective work at its best.)

MATERIALS

- oil-free sunscreen lotion (SPF 15 or higher)
- cup or plate
- cotton swab

- blank piece of white paper
- ultraviolet (UV) "black" light

Note: Black lights are available at hardware stores, lightbulb supply companies, novelty stores, and online. Beware. Not all "black lights" are *real* black lights. Make sure you buy an *ultraviolet* (UV) black light instead of a regular lightbulb that has been painted purple.

PROCEDURE

1. Pour a small amount of sunscreen into a cup or onto a plate.

2. Dip the end of the cotton swab into the sunscreen.

3. Using the cotton swab like a pen, write a message on the paper. (Hint: Use a small amount of sunscreen—so small you can barely see it when you write. If you use too much, it will soak through the paper, and the enemy will be able to read your message. You may have to practice a few times to get it just right.)

4. Let the sunscreen dry.

5. To read your secret message, hold the paper near a fluorescent black light in a dark room.

How does this work?

Black light emits ultraviolet (UV) light. UV light cannot be seen by the human eye. White paper contains brighteners. (So does white clothing.) When exposed to a black light, the brighteners change the ultraviolet light into visible light, and the paper glows. However, sunscreen blocks UV light, so the sunscreen letters appear dark against the white background.

Tired of someone marking up your campaign posters? Tired of seeing yourself with missing teeth, a beard, black eyes, and maybe a horn or two? Tired of long hours of surveillance with no results? Not to worry. Using the products listed below, you can try some high-tech detective work of your own, just like Drake and Nell did.

A) The ultraviolet thief-detection powder that Drake and Nell used to nab Haley in Chapter Eight is available through the following company:

> Shomer-Tec
> www.shomer-tec.com
> P.O. Box 28070
> Bellingham, WA 98228
> tel: (360) 733-6214 fax: (360) 676-5248

B) If you want to try something a little different, there is a fluorescent lotion made especially for kids. It's called GlitterBug Potion and is produced by:

> Brevis Corporation
> www.brevis.com
> 225 West 2855 South
> Salt Lake City, UT 84115
> tel: (800) 383-3377 U.S. and Canada
> fax: (801) 485-2844
> E-mail: info@brevis.com
> (See how it works at www.glitterbug.com)

A Dark and Stormy . . . Mouth: Fluorescence

Imagine it. You're minding your own business, when your mouth suddenly explodes! Tiny lightning bolts flash between your teeth! Thunder rolls! A meteorite crashes! (Well, okay. Maybe it's not that explosive, but it's certainly worth a try.)

MATERIALS

- wintergreen mints (Don't use sugarfree mints, or the experiment won't work.)
- your chompers
- a very dark room with a mirror

PROCEDURE

1. Turn out the lights and wait a minute or two to allow your eyes to adjust to the dark.

2. While watching in the mirror, quickly chomp on a mint with your mouth open.

How does this work?

If you blow up a balloon, you are storing energy in it. If you let go of the balloon, it whizzes around the room, releasing its stored energy. In the same way, when sugar crystals are compressed into a mint, energy is stored. As you break apart the crystals, instead of whizzing around the room, this energy is released as ultraviolet light. Wintergreen transforms the ultraviolet light into visible light in a process called fluorescence.